The WOLF in SHEEP'S CLOTHING

An Aesop's Fable retold by Mark White

Illustrated by Sara Rojo

Raintree

www.raintreepublishers.co.uk
Visit our website to find out more information about Raintree books.

To order:
☎ Phone 0845 6044371
🖹 Fax +44 (0) 1865 312263
🖥 Email myorders@raintreepublishers.co.uk

Customers from outside the UK please telephone +44 1865 312262

Raintree is an imprint of Capstone Global Library Limited,
a company incorporated in England and Wales having its registered office
at 7 Pilgrim Street, London, EC4V 6LB
– Registered company number: 6695582

Art Director: Kay Fraser
Graphic Designers: Emily Harris and Victoria Allen
Production Specialist: Sarah Bennett
Editor: Catherine Veitch
Originated by Capstone Global Library Ltd
Printed and bound in China by Leo Paper Products Ltd

ISBN 978 1 406 24300 0 (paperback)
16 15 14 13 12
10 9 8 7 6 5 4 3 2 1

British Library Cataloguing in Publication Data
A full catalogue record for this book is available
from the British Library.

What is a fable?
A fable is a story that teaches a lesson.
In some fables, animals may talk and
act the way people do. A Greek slave
named Aesop created some of the world's
favourite fables. Aesop's Fables have been
enjoyed for more than 2,000 years.

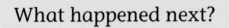

What happened next?

Read the story to find out...

Once there was a clever wolf.

Each night, he watched the farmer lock his
flock of sheep inside a tall fence.

The wolf wanted to get inside and eat
the sheep. But the fence was too high
to jump over.

"How can I get inside?" the wolf
asked himself.

One day, the wolf had an idea. He would dress up as a sheep!

That night, the farmer brought the sheep
home. The wolf slipped into the flock.

The farmer didn't notice anything strange as
the wolf walked past him into the pen.

"Come on," the farmer said. "In you go."

Click! The farmer locked the gate. At last,
the wolf was on the other side of the fence!

The wolf was deciding which sheep to
eat first.

Just then, the farmer came back.

"I need something to eat," the farmer said.

He entered the gate and killed a sheep
for his dinner.

But the sheep he had killed was actually the wolf!

The farmer said to himself, "It is dangerous to pretend to be something you are not."